Mathilde Blind

The Heather on Fire

A Tale of the Highland Clearances

Mathilde Blind

The Heather on Fire
A Tale of the Highland Clearances

ISBN/EAN: 9783744777575

Printed in Europe, USA, Canada, Australia, Japan

Cover: Foto ©Andreas Hilbeck / pixelio.de

More available books at **www.hansebooks.com**

THE HEATHER ON FIRE:

A TALE OF

THE HIGHLAND CLEARANCES.

BY

MATHILDE BLIND.

———◆———

LONDON : WALTER SCOTT, 24 WARWICK LANE,
PATERNOSTER ROW.
1886

DEDICATED

TO

CAPTAIN CAMERON,

WHOSE GLORY IT IS TO HAVE THROWN UP HIS PLACE RATHER THAN PROCEED IN COMMAND OF THE STEAMER "LOCHIEL," WHICH WAS TO CONVEY THE POLICE EXPEDITION AGAINST THE SKYE CROFTERS IN THE WINTER OF 1884.

"THE FOXES HAVE HOLES, AND THE BIRDS OF THE AIR HAVE NESTS, BUT THE SON OF MAN HATH NOT WHERE TO LAY HIS HEAD."

PREFACE.

I SEEM to hear many a reader ask whether such atrocities as are described in " The Heather on Fire " have indeed been committed within the memory of this generation. Let him be assured that this is no fancy picture ; that, on the contrary, the author's aim has been to soften some of the worst features of the heart-rending scenes which were of such frequent occurrence during the Highland Clearances. Many of them are too revolting for the purposes of art ; for the ferocity shown by some of the factors and ground-officers employed by the landlords in evicting their inoffensive tenantry, can only be matched by the brutal excesses of victorious troops on a foreign soil. But even in those cases where no actual violence was resorted to, the uprooting and transplantation of whole communities

of Crofters from the straths and glens which they
had tilled for so many generations must be regarded
in the light of a national crime.

No traveller can have failed to be struck by the
solitude and desolation which now constitute the
prevalent character of the Scottish Highlands.
" Mile after mile," says Macaulay, speaking of Glencoe,
" the traveller looks in vain for the smoke of one hut,
or for one human form wrapped in a plaid, and
listens in vain for the bark of a shepherd's dog, or the
bleat of a lamb.   Mile after mile, the only sound that
indicates life is the faint cry of a bird of prey from
some storm-beaten pinnacle of rock."   His words
might appropriately stand for a description of a
great part of the north of Scotland.   But it was not
always so.   The moors and valleys, whose blank
silence is only broken by the rush of tumbling streams
or the cry of some solitary bird, were once enlivened
by the manifold sounds of human industry and made
musical with children's voices.   The crumbling walls
and decaying roof-trees of ruined villages still bear
witness to the former populousness of many a deserted
glen.   Perhaps these humble remains touch our

feelings more deeply than the imposing fragments of Greek temples and Roman amphitheatres. For it was but yesterday that they were inhabited by a brave, moral, and industrious peasantry, full of poetic instincts and ardent patriotism, ruthlessly expelled their native land to make way for sporting grounds rented by merchant princes and American millionaires.

During a visit I paid to the Isle of Arran in the summer of 1884, I stood on the site of such a ruined village. All that remained of the once flourishing community was a solitary old Scotchwoman, who well remembered her banished countrymen. Her simple story had a thrilling pathos, told as it was on the melancholy slopes of North Glen Sannox, looking across to the wild broken mountain ridges called " The Old Wife's Steps." Here, she said, and as far as one could see, had dwelt the Glen Sannox people, the largest population then collected in any one spot of the island, and evicted by the Duke of Hamilton in the year 1832. The lives of these crofters became an idyll in her mouth. She dwelt proudly on their patient labour, their simple joys, and the kind, helpful ways of them ; and her brown eyes filled with tears as she recalled the day of their expulsion, when the people gathered from all parts of the island to see the last of the Glen Sannox folk ere they went on board the brig that was bound for New Brunswick, in Canada. "Ah, it was a sore day that," she sighed, "when the old people cast themselves down on the sea-shore and wept."

They were gone, these Crofters, and their dwellings laid low with the hill-side, and their fertile plots of corn overrun with ling and heather ; but the stream went rushing on as of old, and as of old the cloven mountain peaks cast their shadow on the valley below whence the once happy people were all gone—gone, too, their dwelling-places, and, to use the touching words of a Highland minister, "There was not a smoke there now." For the progress of civilisation, which has redeemed many a wilderness, and glad-dened the solitary places of the world, has come with a curse to these Highland glens, and turned green pastures and golden harvest-fields once more into a desert.

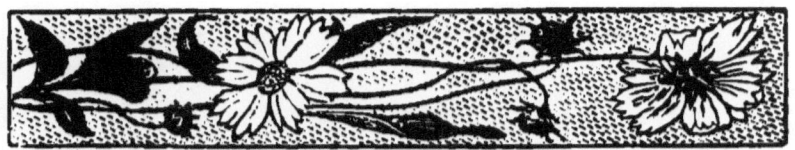

THE HEATHER ON FIRE:
A Tale of the Highland Clearances.

Duan First.

I.

HIGH on a granite boulder, huge in girth,
    Primæval waif that owned a different
        birth
    From all the rocks on that wild coast,
        alone,
Like some grey heron on as grey a stone,
And full as motionless, there stood a maid,
Whose sun-browned hand her seaward eyes did shade
Flinching, as now the sun's auroral motion
Twinkled in milky ways on the grey heaving ocean.

II.

Ah! she had watched and waited overlong ;—
But now as the new sunshine poured along
Heaven's hollow dome, till all its convex blue
Brimmed over as a harebell full of dew—
Yea, now she snatched the kerchief from her hair,
And waved its chequered tartan in the air ;
For all at once she heard o'er ocean's calm
The home-bound fishermen chanting King David's
        psalm.

III.

In stormful straits, where battering craggy heights
Thundered the surf through equinoctial nights,
Off dolorous northern strands where loomed Cape
        Wrath
Red-lurid o'er the sea's unnatural math
Of goodly ships and men, or yet where lone
The Orkneys echoed to the tidal moan,
These men had plied their perilous task and rude,
Wrestling with wind and wave for scantiest liveli-
        hood.

IV.

Now laden they returned with finny spoil
The deep had tendered to their arduous toil ;
Their fishing smacks, with every black sail fanned
By favouring breezes, bore towards the land ;
And in their wake, or wheeling far away,
Or headlong dropping on the hissing spray,
Shrieked flocks of shore-birds, as now hove in sight
Fantastic cliffs and peaks a-bloom with morning
    light.

V.

Ah! dear as is her first-born's earliest lisp
To a young mother, toying with the crisp
Close rings that shine in many a clustering curl
Above the fair brow of her baby girl ;
Or welcome, as when parted lovers meet
Their blissful looks and kisses,—even so sweet
Unto the eyes of those sea-weary men
Gleamed old familiar sights of their own native
    glen :

VI.

The shallow stream wide-straggling on the beach,
That from cleft mountain ridges out of reach
Of aught save eagles, clattered from on high
To water the green strath and then to die
Merged in the deep ; the monstrous rocks that lay
Sharp-fanged like crocodiles agape for prey ;
The mushroom hovels pitch-forked on the strand,
Where browsed the small lean cattle mid the wet
    sea-sand.

VII.

And from her perch the Highland lass had leaped,
Bounding from stone to stone, while still she kept
Her footing on the slippery tangled mass,
Through which her bare, brown, shapely feet did
    pass.
Nor was she now alone on that bleak shore,
For from each hut and corrie 'gan to pour
Women, old men, and children, come to greet
The fishers steering home their little herring-fleet.

VIII.

For now each boat was almost within reach,
Their keels were grating harshly on the beach ;
A rough lad here flung out his rope in coils,
There nets were cast ashore in whose brown toils
Live herrings quivered with a glint like steel,
Which, deftly shovelled into many a creel,
Were carried to the troughs.   And full of joy
The sailor hailed his wife, the mother kissed her
    boy.

IX.

But oh, rejoicing most of any there,
Rejoicing met one fond and faithful pair,
Whose true and tender hearts, tried in love's fire,
Life could not change, howe'er it might conspire
With the revolving, disenchanting years
To turn love's rainbow promises to tears,
And ruthlessly to tear asunder still
What seemed for ever joined by fate and mutual
    will.

X.

Had not nine Aprils with fleet sun and showers,
On wan hill-sides kindled a flame of flowers?
Had not nine harvest moons in sheltered nooks,
Seen the shorn fields piled with the barley stooks,
Since these two lovers in their buoyant youth
Exchanged the vows they kept with stainless
    truth?
Both toiling late and soon, year in, year out,
One longed-for day to bring their marriage morn
    about.

XI.

But toil is long, and oh, man's youth so fleet!
Fleeter love's hours when hands and lips may
    meet!
Weary the moons when they are wrenched apart,
For hope delayed still maketh sick the heart.
And often when the lashing rain would smite
The lowly hut throughout the moaning night,
Beside her bed the girl fell on her knees,
Praying her God for those in peril of the seas.

XII.

But now their nets had drawn great hauls aloft,
And Michael, who had left his inland croft
For female hands to till while he should reap
The fickle harvest of the unsown deep,
Returned not empty-handed to the side
Of her he looked to wed ere Christmastide ;
As thirstily he met those sea-deep eyes,
Where her long love lay hid, a pearl beyond all
    price.

XIII.

A grave, grand Crofter pitted in his pride
Against the niggard soil or veering tide ;
Whose natural ruddy fairness wind and sun
Conspired to dye together of a dun
Unchanging umber—much as though he were
Tarred like his sails for equal wear and tear—
Wherein his eyes' unsullied blue seemed isled,
Clear as two crystal springs by foul things ne'er
    defiled.

2

XIV.

Grave, too, the girl that was to be his bride,
Whose dark head, as she stepped out by his side,
Brushed his red-bearded chin : supple and frail,
She looked a birch tree swaying with the gale ;
And her pale cheeks and shadowy eyes and hair
Seemed veiled by some pathetic brooding care,
But that her ripe lips, with their cranberry red,
A glow of youthful bloom on all her features
    shed.

XV.

With many a " God-speed " from the fishermen,
The lovers left the sea-board for the glen,
Following the devious windings of the burn,
Whose eddying waters flung themselves in turn
O'er heaps of tumbled blocks, or, stilled and deep,
In glassy shallows seemed to fall asleep,
Where, grimly twisted by Atlantic storms,
Grey birks leant over it their pale, distorted forms.

XVI.

A lone, green place, with no live thing around,
No barks, or bleats, or lowings, save the sound
Of running waters, that, with many a fall
And fluid splash, meandered musical ;
Running through months, years, ages, on and on,
Monotonously beneath moon or sun,
With fugitive, ever-recurring chime
Echoing the swift pulsation of the heart of time.

XVII.

A green, lone place for lovers such as these,
Where sitting underneath the birchen trees—
On knolls of tufted moss, whose amber sheen
Seemed rings of sunshine breaking through the
    green—
Hand locked in hand, enlaced and tranced with bliss,
Love's smouldering fire flamed out in one long kiss
Full of the smothered yearning at each heart,
While duty and stern fate kept their two lives
    apart.

XVIII.

There having lingered for a golden space,
Lulled by the burn, face leaning close to face,
How loth soe'er at last they turned away
To follow the steep upland track that lay
Beside the tumbling stream.   For o'er the glade
The hills began to cast a lengthening shade,
And from lone hollows filmy veils of mist
Fell round their furrowed brows in vaporous
    amethyst.

XIX.

And from the height of that green slope awhile
Michael and Mary, leaning 'gainst the stile,
Looked down the long withdrawing upper glen,
The home of patient and laborious men ;
Where it lay spread beneath their loving gaze
Transfigured, glowing to an amber blaze
Poured forth from out the incandescent west,
Where the sun hovered above the purple mountain's
    crest.

XX.

And so the twain cross to the fields of corn
With half their yellow barley yet unshorn,
Where still with rhythmic stroke the reaper walks,
His sickle crackling through the bearded stalks,
While the grain falls in heavy swathes, and then
Bound by brown maids is flung unto the men,
Who shouldering sheaf on sheaf all neatly bound
Stook them in even shocks along the bristling
    ground.

XXI.

And then they pass through meadows soft as sleep
And white with sprinklings of the black-nosed
    sheep,
Where the tall stacks their lengthening shadows fling,
Along the golden green of sun-setting ;
While through the air, in pendulous ebb and rise,
A smoke-like pillar moves athrob with flies,
Myriads of murmuring specks that pulse and quiver
Athwart the moted beam that spans the rushing
    river.

XXII.

There, clustering near the stream in crooked line,
The crofters' steadings, warmly thatched, incline
Brown sloping roofs o'er which rope nets are
  thrown,
And kept in place by many a ponderous stone
Against the winter winds ; and all around
With kale, potatoes, garden-stuff, the ground
Looked like a patch-work counterpane with edges
Of currant bushes and frayed blackberry hedges.

XXIII.

And other farms appeared of their own will
To have got rooted half-way up the hill,
Where mid the wine-red ling they seemed to be
Green islands ringed round by a purple sea ;
And far and wide along the pleasant strath
The air smelt fragrant of the aftermath,
While nimbly darting o'er the new-mown meadows,
Shrill twittering swallows flashed above their
  flashing shadows.

XXIV.

"My glen, my bonnie glen!" the Crofter said,
And reverently bared his tawny head,
As he beheld aglow in sunset's ray
The roof where first he saw the light of day—
The strip of garden, to his infant eyes
Delightful as a nook of Paradise,
Where bees and pigeons murmuring, once to him
Seemed echoes from afar of quiring cherubim.

XXV.

Even, as of yore, there wound the crooked street;
There sprawled small children with bare legs and
      feet;
There on a step stroking her whiskers sat,
Sublimely tolerant, a green-eyed cat;
And there too—in the middle of the road,
Where the tall waggon swayed its creaking load
Of high-piled oats—the cackling hens, a flutter,
Scratching pecked up the grain with fussy haste and
      clutter.

XXVI.

And even as the stately couple stepped
Up the fair clachan, two large collies leaped
Into the street with short sharp barks of joy,
And in their haste knocked a small touzled boy
Into the gutter, where he lay and kicked,
While the dogs dashed at Michael, madly licked
His labour-hardened hands, and tried in vain
To reach his kindly face, then barked and jumped
    again.

XXVII.

And at the loud glad noise an ancient dame
Stepped to the door, and stood with stooping frame,
And left hand warding off the dazzling rays.
Like yellow parchment showed her crumpled face
Scrawled o'er illegibly in runic wise
With time's own handwriting ; and yet her eyes
Scarce matched its age—still young with love and
    teen,
As rain in winter keeps the grass more freshly
    green.

XXVIII.

" Oh mother, mother ! " cried the bearded man,
As hurrying up he took her visage wan
Between his hands, kissing her face and hair,
As it might be a babe's, with tender care ;
Then stooping he passed swiftly through the door
To where right in the middle of the floor
A fire of turf blazed on a flat round stone,
Whose leaping flames all round with equal lustre
    shone.

XXIX.

There Michael's father sat by, the red glare
Touching his silver canopy of hair
Into a fitful brightness, with his proud
Grand head erect, though his strong frame was
    bowed,
Felled at one blow—as when upon some height
A fir, once fronting the confederate might
Of winds from all the compass, on the holt
Falls blasted, cloven in twain by heaven's sheer
    thunder-bolt.

XXX.

So Michael, since he was a lad no more,
Three feeble lives on his strong shoulders bore
Along life's road : for yet in manhood's prime,
His father had come home one winter time
From some fierce battle waged on fields of Spain,
Where he and fellows like him helped to gain
The day for England's king—alas ! for him
That gain was loss indeed :—crippled in life and
   limb,

XXXI.

With right arm gone, on crutches, he returned
Who had gone forth a stalwart man, that burned
With lust for action ; and while still at heart
Life's pulse beat strongly, he was set apart,
Helpless as any log, unfit for toil,   .
Condemned to see the woman drudge and moil,
Doing the man's work and her own beside—
Slaving from night to morn, from morn to eventide.

XXXII.

For she would cut the peat-moss, dig, and plough ;
Would reap the barley-field and milk the cow ;
Would spin and weave the wool her hands did shear
Into stout plaids and comfortable gear ;
Would dye the home-spun cloth and rainproof
    tweed
In hues wrung from the ling and sea-brown weed.
But even the strength her strong love fed at last
Broke with the heavy load on her brave shoulders
    cast.

XXXIII.

For though the heart is willing, even unto death,
The flesh is weak, and fails with failing breath.
Beneath the daily burden's daily strain,
Her work-worn body failed, however fain
She was, despite her aching bones, to keep
The mate and bairns that could not sow or reap,
Yet sorely needed to be housed and fed
Howe'er the sun might sear or wild winds howl
    o'erhead.

XXXIV.

So she broke down at last, however loth,
And her young son now laboured for them both ;
And for the little sister, barely nine,
Who yet would twirl the spindle, coil up twine,
Or take their milch cow to the field to graze :
So, driven by ceaseless tasks, the urgent days
Had waxed and waned, years followed one another,
The lass had left her home, herself now wife and
　　mother.

XXXV.

But honest Michael had not dared to wed
The orphan girl whose dark and stately head
In harvest fields rose first above the rye—
While yet amid the opalescent sky
A tremulous and dilatory light,
Reluctant on the rear of refluent night,
And shuddering through immensities afar
Ethereally flamed the bright and morning star.

XXXVI.

Yea, though her lot was lowly, though the round
Of want's imperious pressure hemmed and bound
The orphan's life with those encircling walls
Wherewith predestined poverty enthralls
And stuns such toiling folk, until they ask
But food and sleep after the long day's task—
Moments she knew when mystical, intense,
The universal soul thrilled through her inner sense.

XXXVII.

Then had she felt what she could ne'er express—
A love, a worship, a sublime excess
Of pure impersonal rapture such as thrills
The lark's breast when his staunchless music fills
Earth, air, and listening heaven ;—but all too soon,
Like flashes of a storm-bewildered moon,
Vanished the gleam—once more a rustic lass,
She sheared the rustling grain, or through the
    rushy grass

XXXVIII.

Wading bare-legged in the chill evening dews,
Drove home the cattle, who, with deep-toned moos,
Snatched yet one last sweet mouthful and yet one
Ere ruminatingly at set of sun
They straggled toward their stalls.   And still so
    well
The maid had served her masters, it befell
That as the years rolled on deep-hearted Mary
From cow-girl was become head of the Castle dairy.

XXXIX.

And patient as her lover, and as brave,
From out her wages yearly she would save
A little hoard of coins, to line the nest
What time their life's love should be crowned and
    blest
In holy wedlock.   Of that day now spoke
Those four at meeting, while braw Michael broke
His fast with porridge, cakes, and barley bree,
By Highland air and hunger seasoned ambrosially.

XL.

But day declined, the lass must say good-bye,
Once more to hasten to her milky kye.
Bending a moment o'er the old man's chair,
Her fresh lips reverently touched his hair,
To whom—her young form vanishing from sight—
The room hath darkened, even as though a light
Were put out suddenly ; for still the old
Warm their chill lives where youth's warm glowing
    loves unfold.

XLI.

And lustily once more that tall pair strode
Along the hilly, devious-winding road,
White in the harvest moon, who from on high
Watched like the night's love-lighted mother eye
Benignly o'er that hill-embosomed glen,
Dotted with little homes of Highland men ;
As though in mercy she would ward and keep
All harm from those that there beneath low rafters
    sleep.

XLII.

Shine, quiet moonlight, shine! Relax, unloose
The sweating peasants' over-laboured thews!
Ease their tired muscles with thy healing balm,
Breathe o'er their brows a pure, infantine calm,
Dissolving all their senses in the deep
Oblivion of immeasurable sleep!
Shine, quiet moonlight, shine! O'er roofs like these
Shed downier peace than falls o'er great kings'
    palaces.

XLIII.

Far o'er the moon-white way the lovers sped,
And in the moonlight showed transfigurèd,
Till looking on each other, their deep eyes
Shone full of love, even as with stars the skies.
Silent amid the silence, hand in hand,
They hardly walked but floated through a land
Whose hills and trees, sheeted in mystic white,
Seemed disembodied shapes floating away in light.

And now the forest with its lichened pines,
Through which the broken moonlight swerving
    shines,
Roofs in the pair, outstepping through the deep
Wet bracken, whence, with sudden upward leap,
Tall antlered creatures start, and stare with eyes
Widely dilated in a wild surprise—
Then at one bound the herd hath fled, as still
As clouds that dreamlike fly athwart an evening hill.

XLV.

And this the bourne where Michael must be gone—
Through here the crested portal leads alone
Down the tall avenue, whose furrowed trees
Have weathered the same tale of centuries
As the square tower and lofty parapet
Of the grim castle, which, as black as jet,   .
Against the moon with massive walls doth stand—
The lordly mansion of the lord of all that land.

3

XLVI.

To him belonged the glens with all their grain;
To him the pastures spreading in the plain ;
To him the hills whence falling waters gleam ;
To him the salmon swimming in the stream ;
To him the forests desolately drear,
With all their antlered herds of fleet-foot deer ;
To him the league-long rolling moorland bare,
With all the feathered fowl that wing the autumn
    air.

XLVII.

For him the hind's interminable toil :
For him he ploughed and sowed and broke the soil,
For him the golden harvests would he reap,
For him would tend the flocks of woolly sheep,
For him would thin the iron-hearted woods,
For him track deer in snow-blocked solitudes ;
For him the back was bent, and hard the hand,
For was he not his lord, and lord of all that land ?

Duan Second.

I.

ROSE now the longed-for, long-delaying hour
　　To which, as towards the sun the sunward flower,
Their hearts had turned though many a year of life,
When Michael should take Mary unto wife.
Long, long before the laggard sun arose
Flushing the hill-sides' freshly fallen snows,
The bride and bridegroom, in their best array,
Footed it to the kirk on this their wedding day.

II.

At home·the neighbours, full of kindly zest,
Prepared the feast for many a wedding guest ;
Swept out the barns and scoured the dusky byres ;
Piled high the peats and kindled roaring fires,
Whose merry flames in golden eddies broke
Round ancient cauldrons crusted o'er with smoke,
Whence an inviting savour steaming rose,
As, slowly bubbling, boiled the meaty barley brose.

III.

Spread was the board ; the various kinds of meat,
Or roast or stew, sent up a savour sweet,
Grateful to Highlanders, whose frugal cheer
Is broth and oatmeal porridge all the year.
But on this happy day no stint there was
For all who liked to come and take their glass
Of the good whisky, and with hearty zest
Drink to the new-wed pair with many a boisterous
        jest.

IV.

From township, bothie, shieling, miles away,
The guests had flocked to grace this festive day :
The shepherd left his fold, the lass her byre,
Old folks their ingle-nook beside the fire,
Mothers their bairns—yea, half the country-side
Turned out to hail the strapping groom and bride ;
And jolly pipers scaled the break-neck passes,
With frolic tunes to rouse the lightsome lads and
    lasses.

V.

Now smoked the feast, now peat-fires cheerier
    burned,
As from the kirk the bridal pair returned ;
And Michael's mother rose from her snug seat,
And came towards the bride with tottering feet,
And tremulous hands outstretched, and sweetly
    spoke
Her welcome : ruddier than her scarlet cloak
The bride's cheek glowed beneath her black silk hood,
As on the threshold of her home she blushing stood.

VI.

Ah ! dear to her that narrow, grey-thatched home,
Where she would bide through all the years to come;
Round which her hopes and memories would entwine
With fondness, as the tendrilled eglantine
Clings round a cottage porch ; where work and love,
Like the twin orbs that share the heavens above,
Would round their lives, and make the days and
    nights
Glad with the steady flame of those best household
    lights.

VII.

Was there no omen, then, no warning thrill,
With curdling dread her warm young blood to chill,
To cast the shadow of a coming doom
Across the sunshine and the tender bloom
Of her new-flowering bliss ?—nor anywhere
A hint of all the sorrow and despair,
The anguish, and the terror, and the strife
Which, earthquake-like, would crush and overwhelm
    her life ?

VIII.

Thank God that no foreboding shadow fell
Across the threshold where love throve so well ;
Nor was there one endowed with second-sight,
To tell of things their present mirth to blight.
No, all were joyous ! Good cheer made them glad,
The whisky gladder still ! Tongues wagged like
    mad !
Full oft drank they the bride and bridegroom's weal,
And merrily played the pipers many a stirring reel.

IX.

And Michael's father, nodding to the bride,
Rapped sharply on the table as he cried,
Seizing the cup in his one trembling hand,
Like some hoar Patriarch of a storied land :
" Lads, here's to Donald's memory ! Mary, lass,
Here's to thy father ! What a man he was !
My brave, God-fearing Donald ! These old eyes
Shall never see his like—so loving, leal, and wise.

X.

"Lads, here's to him ! Aye, well I mind the day
When on the heights of Aldea crouched we lay
For hours amid the furze, and thundering hot
The sun blazed, and we durst not fire a shot,
We of the Forty-Second : up the steep
Like cats we saw the stealthy Frenchmen creep—
Our General, too, asleep ! To ward off flies,
He'd put a sheet of news across his steely eyes.

XI.

" By'r Lord ! if there he didn't take his rest
As sweetly as an infant at the breast.
But when our captain up to him—he woke,
Just raised his head a bit, and answering spoke :
'The Frenchmen coming up the hill ? What then ?
Drive me these Frenchmen down again, my men !'
Aye, and we did so, without more Parlez ;
To hear Sir Arthur, bless your hearts, was to obey.

XII.

" Fluttered our plaids behind us down the hill,
And how our bayonets shone ! I see them still
Flash back the Spanish sunlight ! Oh, the sight,
To see these black French devils taking flight,
And helter-skelter in their hurry run
Backwards with clashing swords ! Then, lads, the fun
Of chasing Johnny Crapaud, as we here
With loud halloos and shouts follow the flying deer.

XIII.

" But needs they must come back ! And, as before,
The General says, 'Why, drive them back once
    more ! ' "
The old man paused, looked round, took a long drain
Of usquebaugh, and said, " Look you, again
Those Frenchmen swarmed more numerous than
    before
Up the hill-side ! Sir Arthur, on being told,
Moved not a muscle, but just calm and cold
As was his wont, he muttered, still quite civil :
' Drive me, I say, these Frenchmen to the devil ! '

XIV.

"And that we did!   By'r Lord, we did that time!"
Some thumped the floor, some made their glasses
    chime,
Some quaffed more whisky as the board they smote
With shouts of bravo!   Rory cleared his throat,
And added calmly, in his deep-toned bass:
"Aye, 'tis like yesterday, my little lass,
Since I saw Donald last;—but few, my dear,
Will mind him that's awa' of all the good folk here.

XV.

"Well, lads, we fired one volley ere we charged,
And by my side the faithful comrade marched,
When in a twinkling—mark you!—Donald Blair
Lap suddenly right up into the air;
As I have seen a noble red deer leap,
Shot by a gillie, then all of a heap
Fall down face foremost—so he struck the sod:
I'd fell the hand that fired the shot, so help me God!

XVI.

" The firing slackened then ; I'd marked him well,
And by-and-by my turn came, when we fell
To fighting hand to hand—I knew him by
The white patch on his nose, and sure 'twas I
That passed my bayonet through him ; so the trick
Was done, you see ; he followed pretty quick
At my poor Donald's heels, the loon ! ah well,
He ne'er went back to France, but like enough to
    hell.

XVII.

" So Donald was avenged—we won the day.
'Tis lang syne now, the brown heads have turned
    grey,
The grey are in their graves; but seems I hear
At whiles brave Donald's laugh so ringing clear,
And see his teeth gleam through his curly beard.
Those were braw fechting days ! Ye'll all have
    heard
Tell on the Forty-Second ? Show us the glen
In Highland or in Island sent not its bonny men !"

XVIII.

The old man's eyes gleamed with young fire again.
" Here's to the lads we left behind in Spain ! "
He cried, and quaffed his bumper with a will.
And now the pipers struck up loud and shrill ;
And while the old sat spinning many a yarn,
The young folk blithely gathered in the barn ;
And with their fun and loud-resounding laughter,
Shook the worm-eaten beams and cobweb-crusted
    rafter.

XIX.

Cheeks flushed, eyes sparkled, hearts beat high and
    fast,
As o'er the floor their feet revolving passed,
Till, to the sound of hornpipes and of reels,
It seemed their hearts went dancing in their heels.
With rhythmic motions now, and face to face,
They tap the shaking boards with natural grace ;
Then, with the wild deer's swiftness, boy and girl
Circling in dizzy maze around each other twirl.

XX.

And as they fling, and cling, and wheel, and pass,
Many a lover lightly hugs his lass ;
And many a village belle and queen of hearts
Makes desperate havoc with her simple arts
'Mid her adoring swains, who, while they shower
Their melting glances on her, glare and glower
Upon their rivals, whom, while meekly sighing,
With many a fervid kick they fain would send
    a-flying.

XXI.

But still among the bonnie dancers there
Michael and Mary were the bonniest pair :
So tall and stately, moving 'mid the rout
Of flushed and panting couples, wrapped about
With the pure glory of love, which seemed to fill
And permeate their features with a still
And tender glow—impassioned yet serene,
The scripture of true hearts revealed in rustic mien.

XXII.

On, on they whirled to many a loud strathspey,
Long after groom and bride had gone away ;
Long after the late half-moon's dwindling light
Had risen grisly on the snowy night,
Through which the wind, in sudden fits and spasms,
Went roaring through the roaring mountain
    chasms,
And then fell silent—with a piercing cry,
Like a sore-hunted beast in its last agony !

XXIII.

But oh, what cared these merry wedding-guests,
With flying pulses and with throbbing breasts,
For all the piping winds and palely snows !—
Their pipes out-played the wind-notes, and their
    toes
Out-whirled the whirling snowflakes, and bright eyes
Did very well instead of starry skies ;
And as the winter night grew drear and drearier,
Music and mountain dew but made them all the
    cheerier.

XXIV.

And so the wedding lasted full three days,
With dance and song kept at a roaring pace,
And drinking no whit slacker; then the feast
Came to an end at last, and many a beast—
Rough Highland sheltie, or sure-footed ass—
Carried them safe o'er stream and mountain pass,
Through treacherous mosses and by darkling wood,
Till safe and sound once more by their own hearths
    they stood.

Duan Third.

I.

EARS had passed on : the ever-rolling
years
    On which man's joys and sorrows,
hopes and fears,
His loves and longings, are swept on and on,
Like airy bubbles sparkling in the sun,
Which, forming in a labouring vessel's wake,
Flash for a moment, in a moment break ;
Frail flowers of foam, dissolving as they quiver,
To sink and rise, and sink upon life's rushing
river.

II.

Once more nine Aprils, with fleet sun and showers,
On wan hill-sides had lit a flame of flowers ;
Once more nine harvest moons in sheltered nooks
Saw the shorn fields piled with the barley stooks,
Since Michael had brought home his dear loved
　　wife,
The faithful partner of his arduous life :
Both toiling late and soon, year out year in,
For the old folk and wee bairns the needful bread
　　to win.

III.

But toil is long—and hard the stubborn strife
Which with the inclement elements for bare life
The Crofter wages; yet for all his ills
Deep-rooted love unto the soil he tills
The stout heart bears ;—as mothers oft are fain
To love those best who cost them sorest pain ;
So do these men, matched with wild wind and
　　weather,
Cling to their tumbling burns, bleak moors, and
　　mountain heather.

4

IV.

And lo ! once more it was the time of year
When berries crimson and green leaves grow sere ;
When bluebells shelter numb, belated bees,
And on the outstretched arms of wayside trees
Dangle long wisps of oats, whose casual grain
The thievish sparrows plunder, as the wain
Creaks slowly, lurching sideways, to the croft,
Whose sheaves, by stout arms tossed, are stored in
    barn and loft ;—

V.

That time of year when, smoke-like, from the deep
Atlantic ocean, fast ascending, sweep
Innumerably the rain-burthened clouds,
Taking the sun by storm, and with dim crowds
Confusing heaven, as, flying from the gale,
They blur the lineaments of hill and dale,
Till, dashed on giddy peak and blasted scaur,
Their waters breaking loose, crash in one long
    downpour.

VI.

A drear autumnal night ! The gusty rain
Drums on the thatch ; the tousled birches strain,
Bending before the blast ; and far and wide
The writhen pines roar like a roaring tide,
With which the tumult of the troubled stream
Mingles its rumbling flood : a night to dream
Of dire shipwrecks and sudden deaths at sea—
Yet here, 'neath lowly cot, all sleep most peacefully.

VII.

All sleep but Mary, hushing in her arm
The child whose moans now mingle with the storm
And now fall silent, as his curly head
Nestles against her breast, that burns to shed
The warmth of life into her ailing bairn,
O'er whom her eyes compassionately yearn
With love, such as some master genius fine
Limned in her namesake's eyes, bent o'er the child
    divine.

VIII.

Yea, Mary watched alone, while round her lay
The nut-brown heads of children, and the grey
Deep-furrowed brows of age : now and again,
In the brief pauses of the hurricane,
She caught their rhythmic breathing through the
     thick
Laborious cough and panting of the sick
And feverish child, who now and then made moan—
" Oh, mother, mother dear ! take off that heavy
     stone."

IX.

" Aye, aye," she crooned, stifling a heavy sigh ;
" Aye, aye, my precious darlin', mother 'll try."
And all the night by the red peat-fire's glare,
As many a night before of carking care,
With healing warmth she eased the poor child's ache,
And with sweet cooling drinks his thirst did slake.
At last the racking, troublous cough did cease,
And dozing off towards dawn, he slumbered more
     at ease.

X.

The tempest too lulled suddenly : a swound
As of spent forces hushed the wuthering sound
And tumult of the elements ; wan and grey
In the eastern heavens broke the irresolute day
Still pale and tearful, as the close-veiled sun
Like one who fears to see the havoc done
Peered furtively ; his first and faltering ray
Hailed by a lark's clear voice hymning the new-
    born day.

XI.

A poor caged lark ! But as the exultant note
Burst from the little palpitating throat
Of the imprisoned songster, the dull yoke
Of care that seemed to stifle Mary broke
In a hot flood of tears ; yea, hope once more,
Like a tall pillar of fire, shone before
Her groping steps—the bird's voice seemed to tell
Her listening, anxious heart all would be well, be
    well.

XII.

"Yea, all would yet be well," she murmured; "soon,
With this first quarter of the hunter's moon
Father would come back from the seas, and bring
His gains wherewith to buy so many a thing
Sore needed by the bairn!"   Therewith she rose
More comforted at heart, and tucked the clothes
Warmly around the child, and softly kissed
The little sleeper's thin, brown, closely curled-up fist.

XIII.

And lifting his moist curls, she faintly smiled,
Remembering how last June her ailing child,
As blithe and bonnie as the other twin,
His sister Mary, had come toddling in,
Ruffled and rosy, pressing to his breast
With chubby fingers a forsaken nest,
From which the startled lark had fled in fear,
When 'mid the falling swathes the mowers' scythes
        rang near.

XIV.

But he had rescued it from being crushed
By trampling feet, and eager-eyed and flushed
Had toddled to the cottage with its shy,
Poor half-fledged nestling, that did feebly cry
For food and warmth and mother's folding wing ;
But lovingly he tended the wee thing—
And lo ! it lived, ceasing to pine and fret :
In narrow cage it sang, sweet Michael's cherished
    pet.

XV.

The song aroused the household.   One by one
They rose to do their taskwork with the sun ;
All but the aged woman, now too sore
To leave her bed, or labour any more,
Save with her hands, which still found strength to
    knit
Warm stockings for her son.   Old Rory lit
His pipe, and bending o'er the smouldering fire,
Piled on the well-dried peats and made the flames
    leap higher.

XVI.

Fair Ranza hurried to her dear-loved cow,
Shobhrag, the primrose-hued, that with a low
Of deep content greeted the little maid,
Who bade her a good day, and fondly laid
A soft pale cheek against her shaggy side ;
Then pressing the full udders, sat astride
On her small three-legged stool, and watched the
    white
Warm stream of milk filling her pail with keen
    delight :

XVII.

Yet took great care not to take more than half,
Nor rob the little, cuddling, week-old calf
That stood near by—a glossy golden brown,
Most like a chestnut roughly tumbled down,
When its smooth burnished kernel seems to swell
And burst athwart the trebly-cloven shell—
Whose limpid eyes, pathetically meek,
From their mute depths unto the gentle child did
    speak.

XVIII.

And bare-legged ruddy Ion, whistling shrill,
Scampered across the grass all wet and chill,
And littered with brown leaves and berries red,
While as he brushed the hedge its brambles shed
Brief showers upon him, as with prying look
He keenly searched each ditch and hidden nook
For a scarce egg or two, which now and then
Was laid safe out of sight by some secretive hen.

XIX.

And Mary, bending o'er the peat-fire's glare,
Its bright light dancing on her crispy hair
And white face worn with watching, yet so grand
Lit with those eyes of hers, turned with one hand
The well-browned oat-cakes, while her other one
Had hold of little Maisie, whose bright fun
Was kept in check by whispers from her mother,
Not to disturb or wake the little sleeping brother.

XX.

At last they gathered round the humble fare,
The youngest child repeating the Lord's prayer
With broken baby tones and bended head :
" Give us," she lisped, " this day our daily bread,"
When a loud hurried knocking at the door
Startled the little circle ; even before
They well knew how, into the room there broke
A hurried, flurried group of scared, distracted folk,

XXI.

Wild, panic-stricken neighbours, blanched with
    dread.
How helpless looked the strong !   Discomfited,
Like men from field-work driven by sudden foe
Who yet instinctive clutched their spade or hoe !
And unkempt wives anomalously dressed
With querulous infants huddled to the breast ;
Showing, in quivering lip and quailing eye,
The inevitable stroke of swift calamity.

XXII.

Yet ere one spoke, or could have said a word,
Mary had waved them back : " Nay, by the Lord,
Not here, not here," she whispered hoarse and low ;
" My child is sick—the sleep he's sleeping now
Is worth a life ; " then with a pleading sign
She to the old man's care seemed to resign
Her little ones, and softly closed the door,
Bracing each quivering nerve for some dire grief in
    store,

XXIII.

And walked slow-footed to the outer gate,
'Gainst which she leant her body like a weight ;
And with dry lips, low querying, barely sighed—
" Michael ? The tempest ? " But a neighbour cried,
One of her kin, who grasped her round the waist—
" No, no, look yon ! " And with bare arm upraised
She pointed up the glen, whence drifting came
Dark clouds of rolling smoke lit by red tongues of
    flame.

XXIV.

And through the rolling smoke a troop of men
Tramped swiftly nearer from the upper glen ;
Fierce, sullen, black with soot, some carrying picks,
Axes, and crowbars, others armed with sticks,
Or shouldering piles of faggots—to the fore
A little limping man, who cursed and swore
Between each word, came on post-haste ; his hand,
Stretched like a vulture's claw, seemed grabbing at
    the land.

XXV.

" The deil a one of all the lot shall stay ;
They've a' been warned—I'll grant no more delay ;
So let them e'en be smoked from out their holes,
To which the stubborn beggars stick like moles,
Cumbering the ill-used soil they hack and scratch,
And call it tillage !   Silly hens that'd hatch
Their addled eggs, whether they will or no,
Are beaten off, and sure these feckless fules maun go."

XXVI.

So on from glen to glen, from hut to hut,
The hated factor came with arrogant strut
And harsh imperious voice, and at one stroke,
Of house and home bereft these hapless folk,
Bidding all inmates to come forth in haste :
For now shall their poor dwellings be laid waste,
Their thatch be fired, walls levelled with the leas,
And they themselves be shipped far o'er the wide,
    wild seas.

XXVII.

Thus through his grasping steward bids the chief,
In whom hereditary, fond belief
Honours the proud head of their race—the man
Whose turbulent forbears their devoted clan
Had served in bloody wars, nor grudged to yield
Their lives for them in many a battle-field :
But in these latter days men's lives are cheap,
And hard-worked Highlanders pay worse than
    lowland sheep.

XXVIII.

And so that he unstinted may abide
In all the pomp and power of lordly pride,
Riot in lawless loves, or, if he please,
Have a refreshing change of palaces ;
Or softly warmed in scented orange bowers,
Shun his moist land of mist and mountain showers,
The far-off master hath declared his will,
To have the Crofters swept from every dale and hill.

XXIX.

Ah ! sore's the day to those unhappy folk,
Whose huts must fall beneath the hammer's stroke,
As now the thud of heavy trampling feet
Draws close and closer to their village street ;
Where, hurrying aimlessly, some wildly stray,
While others stand and stare in blank dismay,
And with the sudden shout—" They come !   They
    come ! "
The neighbours rush in fear, each to his threatened
    home.

XXX.

But one, still grasping Mary by the waist,
Abode with her, and said : " Haste, woman, haste !
Let's get the old man and the bairns away,
And whatsoe'er of goods and gear we may,
Before the factor's men break in, and fling
Your bedding in the road and everything
Ye'se bought right dear, and pots and pans and a'
Lie ruined past the mending, broken by their fa'."

XXXI.

But Mary, answering with 'bated breath,
" Ah ! d'ye forget our child nigh sick to death,
And the old bedridden mother ? "—even before
Her tremulous lips could add a syllable more,
A voice smote on her ear, most like the screech
Of some fell bird of prey than human speech,
That bade her, at the law's resistless call,
To clear out quickly, bag and baggage, once for all.

XXXII.

And Mary clasped her hands and raised her eyes,
And with a sudden throb of sharp surprise
She knew the little man who, years gone by,
When she was but a lass who kept the kye—
A bare-legged lassie, but most fair and slim,
Like a young poplar swayed at the wind's whim—
Had come a-courting, and with fierce suit dunned
The maiden for her love, while she him loathed and
    shunned.

XXXIII.

She knew the man, and a quick searing red
Burned cheeks as wan as hueless petals shed
By wind-nipped flowers in autumn. "Lord," she
    cried,
" Ha' mercy ! 'tis Dick Galloway," and eyed
The factor for a while ; then sighing said—
" There's Michael's mother, she's now been a-bed
A weary while ; ah, sir, she is that old
That if she's moved, for sure she'll die of cramp
    and cold."

Then with a break and pleading change of tone,
She pointed o'er her shoulder with a moan
As of a cushat dove in forest deeps—
" My child's been sick, sir ; now, thank God, he
    sleeps.
To drag him out into the gousty glen
Would be sheer murder !   Oh, come ben, come ben,
And see him smile so sweetly where he lies,
'Most like one of God's angels up in Paradise.

XXXV.

" Ye see, if ye'll but bide a little span,
Michael 'll be back, and he's a canny man
For rare devices, and will surely find
A way to shelter them from rain and wind ;
And we'll go quiet and make no lament,
Though me and Michael's always paid the rent
Howe'er we pinched oursel's when times were bad ;
But now ye ken my plight, come see the curly
    lad."

5

XXXVI.

" Plague take the woman, what a mighty fuss
'Bout a bedridden hag and sickly cuss !
D'ye think, dem, I'll stand jawing at this rate
About sick brats at every beggar's gate?
Time's money's worth," the lowland factor sneered ;
And with a vicious gnawing of his beard,
And something of a leer and bantering whine,
" Ye're not so saucy, lass, as was your wont lang
    syne.

XXXVII.

" Ye mind," he hissed, lowering his voice, " I'se bet,
What a big fool ye made of me ; and yet,
Mary, you were a bigger !   Down I went
In the wet grass right on my knees, and spent
My breath in sighs, and, damn me ! all ye'd say
Was, with a loud guffaw, ' Dick Galloway,
For shame, get up, get up, man ! '   Then I swore
You'd rue it, as you have, and shall do more and
    more.

XXXVIII.

"Come, come, time's up ! Clear out of this, I say !
Here, lads, come hither ; help to clear away
This stinking rubbish heap—some of ye chaps
Here lend a hand, clear out this woman's traps.
Of all these dirty huts the glen we'll sweep,
And clear it for the fatted lowland sheep."
Then, with a mocking bow and limping gait,
Left Mary standing there—dumb by the rustic gate.

XXXIX.

"Cowards !" she cried, with a fierce flash of light
In her big eyes, and reared to her full height,
And waved them back as might some warrior queen,
Full-armed and fearless, of her people seen
Foremost upon the ramparts as the foe
Scales her fair walls before their overthrow—
Yea, even with such an air the woman stood :
"Cowards !" she cried once more, "thirst ye for
    children's blood ? "

XL.

Her regal presence and her flashing eyes,
Raised as in supplication to the skies,
Awed even these surly men, who still delayed
To shove her back, and make a sudden raid
Upon her cottage ;—brutal as they were,
The motherhood that yearned through her despair
Awed them a moment—but a moment more
They'd hustled her aside and tramped towards the
      door.

XLI.

Swifter than they—yea, at a single bound,
She swooped above her child's bed, wrapped him
      round
In a thick plaid, and clasped him to her breast,
And panting—" Father, see ye to the rest,
So help me God I can't," she, clutching hold
Of Maisie's hand, strode out into the cold ;
And on a fir uprooted by the gale
Sat down, and hushed the child that 'gan to hoarsely
      wail.

XLII.

Meanwhile the men fell to their work and broke
The rough-cast walls with many a hammer stroke ;
Pulled down strong beams, set the mossed thatch
    on fire,
While Ranza, quivering, flew towards the byre
To save their cow and calf ; and the young son
Of seven seized what he could lay hands upon,
And dragged it in the roadway, for the lad
Knew well 'twas all the wealth his hard-worked
    father had.

XLIII.

And ancient Rory, tottering on his crutch,
Tried all in vain with his one hand to clutch
And lift his palsied wife, who could not hear
His hurried words, all tremulous with fear,
With which he tried to rouse her—all her moan,
A peevish whimper to be left alone,
Till 'mazed, he hobbled off in wild suspense,
Shouting for neighbours' help to bear the old wife
    hence.

XLIV.

Where all was tumult and confusion, where
Shrill cries and wild entreaties filled the air,
And breathless folk pushed wildly to and fro,
They hardly heeded one another's woe.
Long, long it seemed ere Rory's perilous plight
Brought him a helping hand—oh, curdling sight!
Too late, too late!—blankets and bedding blazed
Around the poor old soul, whose skinny arms
    upraised

XLV.

Hacked feebly 'gainst the flames that rose and fell
Hissing and crackling round her. " I'm in hell!"
She mumbled crazily, and stared with dim,
Lack-lustre eyes, struggling with palsied limb
To fly but could not : with his desperate roar,
It seemed the strength of by-gone days once more
Surged through the old man's shrunken veins ; he
    caught
The woman up and bore her hence with horror
    half distraught.

XLVI.

And laid her by the wayside, where her gear
Hissed on the heather ; like a village Lear
His eyes rolled maddening, while some neighbours
    came,
And flinging water on the greedy flame,
They quickly quenched it—but as quickly, oh !
That other flame went out, which here below,
No skill of man hath learned to light again :
Eyes closed, heart stopped, shut fast and locked on
    human pain.

XLVII.

Yet where so many suffered one more wail
Of anguish scarce was heeded !   Rang the dale
With lamentation and low muttering wrath,
As homestead after homestead in the strath,
As hut on hut perched tip-toe on the hills,
Or crouched by burn-sides big with storm-bred rills,
Blazed up in unison, till all the glen
Stood in red flames with homes of ousted Highland
    men.

XLVIII.

And through the dire confusion and the smoke
From burning byres, the cattle roaring broke,
And mad with terror, rushed down from the fells ;
Whole flocks tore bleating onwards, with the yells
Of furious dogs behind them ; whins and trees
Caught fire, and boughs fell crackling on the leas,
And smouldering rafters crashed, and roofs fell in,
And showers of wind-blown sparks high up in air
    did spin.

XLIX.

Distracted, stunned, amazed, the hurrying folk
Sway to and fro ; some harness to the yoke
The loudly whinnying horses, and on van
Or cart, in desperate haste, toss what they can
Of their scant household goods : clothes, bedding,
    chairs,
Spades, hoes, and herring-nets, and such like wares ;
And high atop of all, well nigh despairing,
Wives,   mothers,   children—howling,   weeping,
    swearing.

L.

Here a bold shepherd leaps from rock to rock,
And vainly calls his wildly scattering flock ;
Caught some in burning bushes, or on high
Shown motionless, as marble 'gainst the sky,
Where on some jutting shelf a step amiss
Will hurl them headlong down the precipice.
There, at their peril, clambering cottars seek
To save their precious crops, half stifled with the
    reek.

LI.

But women-folk and children chiefly throng
Helpless about the pathways, since the strong
And able-bodied tarry yet at sea,
Netting the herrings which innumerably
Swim in the merry moonlight ; and, perchance,
While round their keels the silvery waters dance,
Their hearts fly homewards to the huts even then
A-blazing up by hundreds through their native
    glen.

LII.

Yea, all that night about the winding strath—
On brown hill-side and giddy mountain path,
Or where, on dolorous moor and blanching mere,
The dark mist lolled and floated, far and near,
Reddening the river chafed by granite blocks,
The drear ravines, the vapour-shrouded rocks,
And realms wind-haunted—hung that awful light
Of huts and flaming farms ensanguining the night.

LIII.

And ever, as procession-like on high
Swiftly across the wind-tormented sky
The wingèd clouds, crossing from sea to sea,
Rolled o'er the mountain-valley, suddenly
Their livid masses stricken with the glare
Kindled a wrathful crimson, till the air
Seemed to take fire, infected from below,
And earth from heaven itself to catch the unnatural
    glow.

LIV.

And all that lurid night, beside the stream,
With many a wind-snapped pine and blackened
  beam
Hurrying to seaward in the fitful glare
Of blazing roofs and rafters, Mary's care
Was centered on the child upon her knee,
Who gasped, convulsed, in his last agony,
Close to the burden of the life beneath
Her heart—that battle-field of wrestling life and
  death.

LV.

And round her lay her little ones, the shawl
Snatched from her neck a covering for them all—
Where half hid in her gown the nestling things
Showed, as through feathers of maternal wings
The yellow heads of new-hatched chickens peep ;
Yet 'mid confusion calm, they slept the sleep
Of innocents, while watchful mother eyes
Shone o'er them fair as stars flickering through
  stormy skies.

LVI.

The air blew chillier as faint streaks of grey
Broadened towards that mystic time of day
Which oftenest ushers in the feeble cry
Of new-born babes, and hears the last good-bye
Faltered from dying lips; even at that hour
When close-shut petals feel the living power
And thrill of light, the child, with gasping breath,
Shuddered convulsed, and shrank as from the frost
   of death.

LVII.

Then suddenly his writhing limbs relaxed,
The fair, transparent features slowly waxed
Crescent in beauty, and, with nameless awe
Dilating, glowed the eyes, as if they saw
Dawning upon the unfathomable night
And dumb abysms of death, light within light
Shining prophetic on those infant eyes,
Limpid as mountain meres, that glass the starry
   skies.

LVIII.

Like to a drop of morning dew that shone
In momentary lustre and is gone;
Like to a new-lit taper whose fair light
A sudden gust hath quenched ere fall of night;
Like to a fresh-blown lily which the storm
Hath broken ere its time, the flower-like form
Of the fair child lay on its mother's knee,
Unconscious of her sharp, shrill cry of agony,

LIX.

"Oh, Michael, oh, my son!" The piercing wail
Of human grief went echoing on the gale
That sobbed about the pine tops. Howling bayed
The dogs, as if they also mourned the dead;
Then keenly sniffed the air, and barked and leaped
About the woman's skirts. The children wept.
Steps crackled on the leaves. And like a dart
Straight aimed, flew Michael, straining Mary to his
    heart.

LX.

Lo, all her pent-up anguish, all her fears,
Then broke their flood-gates in a storm of tears
Upon her husband's shoulder; with her arms
Locked closely round him, the fell night's alarms,
The home in ashes laid, the sick and old
Relentlessly thrust forth into the cold
Autumnal night—yea, all the pain and trouble
Seemed bearable to her, now that her heart was
    double.

LXI.

Few were his words. What comfort was in speech?
The news had smitten Michael on the beach,
Where late at night he landed.   For a cloud
Of densely rolling smoke hung like a shroud
On the familiar cliffs and well-known bay,
Till the bewildered mariners lost their way
Even in broad noon, but won the shore at night,
Piloted by the flames that flashed from vale and
    height.

LXII.

Oh, ghastly home-coming! Oh, cruel blow!
To find their levelled walls and huts laid low;
Their crofts destroyed, their stacks of fragrant hay
Devoured of greedy flames or borne away
By all the winds of heaven. Oh, harrowing sight!
Sore labour's fruits all wasted in a night;
The banished clansmen hurrying to the shore,
To sound of pipes that wail, Farewell for evermore.

LXIII.

They fly and turn not on the hireling band,
That unresisting drives them from their land.
Dowered with the lion's strength, like lambs they go,
For saith the preacher: "God will have it so.
Therefore, lest worse befall them, lest they yell
Hereafter from the burning pit of Hell,
Let them in judgment for their sins go hence,
Nor vainly strive, poor folk, against God's
    providence."

Duan Fourth.

I.

HIGH among sea-bleached rocks, and bleached as they,
Naked to summer storm, to wintry day,
Unroofed and windowless, a ruined keep
Tottered, suspended o'er the turbulent deep,
That evermore with hungry lap and moan
Gnawed worrying at the bald precipitous stone,
Whose shrubless gaunt anatomy defied
The siege and ruthless onset of the battering tide.

II.

Here it was rumoured, once from furthest Thule
Tall Vikings landed and had fixed their rule,
Harrying the Gaelic people. Here, they said,
One, yet red-handed, forcibly had wed
A slaughtered chieftain's child. White as sea-foam,
He bore the bride up to his eagle home,
Whose hollow vaults echoed the huge carousals
In celebration of those terrible espousals.

III.

But in the dead of night the bride arose,
And noiselessly as the pale drifting snows,
The two-edged sword of him, who, drenched with
    wine,
Slept there, she brandished in the dim moonshine,
And sheathed it in his heart ; then where he lay
Cursed him with a strange curse and fled away :
That curse which for long centuries had preyed
Upon those grisly walls, the credulous sea-folk said.

IV.

To these ill-omened ruins, where all rank
And blistering weeds grew thickly 'mid the dank
Coarse grass and thistles,where the flat-mouthed toad
Squatted, where foxes found secure abode,
Where whooping owls with lidless eyes did stare,
And fluttered bats athwart the dusky air
Shot shuttlewise—even thither Michael bore
Mary, and her sore pangs at his own vitals tore.

V.

For in these ruins, where the hunted beast
Burrowed secure, the outcasts hoped at least
The factor's gang would never track their prey.
With breathless haste the Crofter cleared away
The mouldering rubbish, and with infinite care,
On the hard pillow of the ruinous stair
He propped the dear dark head of her whose spent
Attenuated frame with coming life was rent.

VI.

And to the barren moorland waste forlorn,
Treeless—but for a solitary thorn
That, lightning-stricken and bereft of leaf,
Stood like a gallows waiting for its thief—
The little children went, and blue with cold
And hunger, searched upon the gusty wold
For the spare rust-brown ferns and shrivelled heather
To ease their mother's bones in place of flock and
    feather.

VII.

Their father meanwhile knocked a stancheon
Into some rotten chinks, and thereupon
Stretched a tarred sail across the corner where
His wife lay shivering in the inclement air
Whistling through hole and cranny; from the ground
Sought waifs and strays, and by a godsend found
A piece of solid drift-wood, unawares,
Mayhap, of smugglers left, there hiding perilous
    wares.

VIII.

And with much coaxing of the spitting fuel,
That seemed to wage a sort of spiteful duel
With the recoiling flames, the fitful spark
Flared up at last and wavered through the dark,
As blowing with strong lungs to fan the blaze,
Michael, with new-ploughed furrows in his face,
Stooped over it, to grill the caller herring,
While flameward to their death the flurried moths
    came whirring.

IX.

Then with a mother's tenderness he fed
The shivering, fretful children, and like lead
Their lids fell to, even while the small white teeth
Munched the sore-needed food, as with a sheath
Slumber encompassed them.   The weary souls,
Like little foxes snuggling in their holes,
Lay close around the fire with curled-up toes,
Warmed by the bickering flames and deaf to all
    their woes.

X.

Deaf to the rising blast that rushed and beat
Against the walls—to volleying hail and sleet
Rattling like grapeshot—to the breakers' boom
That right beneath them in the hollow gloom
Seemed plucking at the everlasting rocks
With such terrific and reiterate shocks
Of crashing seas—deaf as the very stones
To lashing winds and waves mixed with their
    mother's groans.

XI.

And as the tempest rose, and as the night
Grew wild and wilder, in the topmost height
Of heaven the sundering cloud-gates showed above
Where the white moon was fleeing like a dove
Before the wrack, or like a living soul
Escaped the body's ponderous control,
And launched into eternity—even so
Her weltering light appeared to Michael in his woe,

XII.

Where, gripped with pain and ineffectual rage,
And helpless as a lion in his cage,
He paced the roofless chamber, or would start
Into the storm to ease his bursting heart.
And rushing forth he in the transient blaze
Of moonlight met his father face to face
Chopping a way athwart the baffling gale,
His hair and matted beard hoar with the rattling
    hail.

XIII.

His father?—nay, not this man—but some vain
Hallucination his distempered brain
Had conjured up from darkness ! Aye, some fell
And shocking mask that mimicked but too well
The venerable head ! Oh, dread surmise !
He knew this form, though from the wandering eyes
A stranger stared, and verily knew not him.
Michael grasped at the wall ; all seemed to turn
    and swim,

XIV.

As, stumbling o'er the threshold, wild and worn,
His face bedaubed with soot, his garments torn,
The old man shook himself, then looked around,
And seeing the children curled up on the ground,
Went painfully down on one knee, and spread
His horny palm towards the fire, that shed
An opal glow ; then, dropping to the earth,
Laughed hoarsely to himself—"Aye, here's a bonnie
    berth.

XV.

" A pretty night, sir, this ! The moon's at full,
That makes the winds go daft, a man from Mull
Told me in private ! 'Tis a rare strathspey
The merry piper's playing ; but, I say,
A drop of whisky, lad ! I've come from far,
And yon—come closer, lad—yon's bloody war."
But his mad ramblings here were cut in twain
By madder hurly-burly of wind-smitten rain.

XVI.

" Happen you haven't heard puir Scotland, lad,
Is done for quite ?   Oh, Lord ! the times are bad.
The French we used to drub now drub us, rob,
Kill, burn the very women ! "   And a sob
Throttled the old man's utterance.   " Oh, the
    shame !—
Our braw lads ran away—ran, sir, like tame,
Pale-livered sheep or rabbits in hot flight !
Had I not left some limbs in Spain, *I'd* make them
    fight.

XVII.

" Aye, there's the trouble ! I've lived overmuch.
Earth's sick of me," and waving his old crutch
Above his head he muttered—" Fire and flood
Fight 'gainst our lads now they are made of wood,
And jointed cunningly to look like men
But bloodless.   So they're burning in the glen,
But I, ye ken, I'm of the Forty-Secon' !
I've served my country well as it has me, I'se
    reckon."

XVIII.

And therewith burst into a husky song
Of doughty Highland deeds, and, crazed with wrong,
Dozed off, nor knew how busy death was there,
Nor that as his new grandchild felt the air
And edge of the inhospitable night,
It shuddered back from life's brink in affright,
Dragging its mother after—where she lay
Like to a gallant ship that dwindling drifts away,

XIX.

Merged in the dim obliterating line
Where heaven and ocean seem to intertwine
Their separate elements. Oh, crushing grief,
With Mary's life Michael's was fain to leave,
Who grasped his head with both his hands as though
To ward off the inevitable blow,
And keep his reeling sense and staggered brain
From breaking down beneath the accumulating
    pain,

XX.

As had his wretched father's !   " Oh, my own
Puir love," he cried, " oh, leave me not alone !
Would I could die with thee, or give my life
For thine, my little lass, my murdered wife !
The Lord have mercy on us !" and the strong
Man shuddered with his sobs, and fiercely clung
To her who sighed, " I'm going with my dears,
Watch thou the bairns that's biding in this vale of
     tears."

XXI.

Crushing her freezing hand in his, the flight
Of hours passed by unheeded, and the night,
With all her winds loud wailing, lapped him round,
And with her own his misery did confound.
Unhappy wretch, not even to mourn his dead
Might he watch unmolested by the bed
Of his life's only treasure ; yea, even then
On his great grief they burst, the great Lord's
     hireling men.

XXII.

Had they not scoured the country far and wide,
The forest maze and crevissed mountain-side,
The wave-bored cavern by the sounding shore,
And haunts of sea-fowl, searching for a score
Or two of fugitive distracted men,
Whose hoary memories hugged their native glen,
As ivy climbing round some king of oaks
Cleaves to and breaks with it beneath the wood-
  man's strokes ?

XXIII.

And by the faint light breaking through a chink
Of the grey ruin tottering on the brink
Of the bleached headland, lo ! the men of law,
By tortuous tracks, had crept to where they saw
The treacherous gleam ; and one among their band,
Even in the name of him who owned that land,
Bade them come on, nor waste their time, for, dem !
The tide was rising, nor would surely wait for them.

XXIV.

Therewith they burnt the heather and the ferns
Gathered and slept on by those weary bairns;
Put out the fire, and tore the sail away,
Where, smooth as in her blooming maiden day—
Like some fair image on a sculptured tomb,
Within a hushed cathedral's mystic gloom—
Recumbent with her infant at the breast,
The large-limbed mother lay in monumental rest.

XXV.

With painful steps slow winding round and round,
Down curving tracks, they gained the burial-ground,
Where some few furlongs from the sea it lay
Upon a slope, acquainted with the spray ;
And where behind it, far receding, rose
Cloud-shouldering pinnacles with maiden snows
Begirt, and luminous with evanescent
Gleams of the casual sun, storm-quenched and still
    renascent.

XXVI.

Within the shadow of the hills o'erhead,
Within the sound of sea-waves lay the dead.
Here, thickly planted, leant the moss-grown stones,
And kept old names green over mouldering bones ;
Or billowy ridges simply marked the spot
Where paupers rested whom even death forgot ;
And crippled thorns and weeping birchen trees
Rustled in conclave of the flight of centuries.

XXVII.

Yea, here, even here, where their forefathers slept,
The children lifted up their voice and wept,
Lamenting as the Israelites of old
In Babylon.   Here, among graves, behold
The desolate folk that congregating swell
To bid their native land a long farewell—
To bid their people's dust a last good-bye,
Wetting with tears that earth where they may never
    lie.

XXVIII.

But lo, all swerved aside, as through the throng
The little funeral party moved along,
All save three mourners, motionless and grey,
With covered faces crouching by the way ;
For all knew Michael, honoured in the strath,
And in compassion mutely cleared a path,
As on his back he and another bore
Sail-shrouded on a plank the wife who was no
    more.

XXIX.

The staggering children, motherless and worn,
Followed, the least one of the eldest borne ;
All meekly, by his little grandson led,
The old man shuffled after—his wild head
Nodding perpetually filled even with awe
The sorrowing folk he passed—but when he saw
So many of his people gathered there,
Returning reason broke on madness of despair.

XXX.

And more and more he came to understand,
As by the new-dug grave he saw them stand,
In which—a shamrock-leaf of lives—were laid
Mother and new-born babe and winsome maid,
Even Ranza—Mary's first-born—she whose brave
Heart forced her staggering footsteps to the grave,
Where she had dropped convulsed, her innocent life
As sorely done to death as by a butcher's knife.

XXXI.

Compassion moved their bowels.   Not an eye
But ran with tears.   Michael's alone were dry.
His heart had rained sorrow unspeakable
On his wife's body ; now an empty well
Seemed drained to the last drop.   But even before
The solemn prayers were ended, from the shore
The factor's gang came pouncing on their prey,
And hounded them with threats of handcuffs to the
    bay.

XXXII.

For many there with sobs and bitter moans
Were clinging round the thorn trees and the stones :
More desperate than any, Rory clave,
Frenzied in turn and fawning, to the grave
Of the Mackinnons.   "I shall stay," he cried,
"With mine own people! Where my forebears
    died,
The good, God-fearing folk, years upon years,
There Rory too will die and mix his dust with
    theirs."

XXXIII.

And then with humbly supplicating mien
Begged and entreated like a frightened wean—
"No, no, ye won't begrudge a little span
Of ground wherein to bury an old man
Four score and over, who will not, for sure,
Long cumber earth that is not for the poor?"
And low he grovelled 'mid the tomb-stones there,
Brushing the long rank grass with his white float-
    ing hair

XXXIV.

He might as well have pleaded with the sea
When, even as then, the surf rolls angrily,
Raging against its bourne. Deaf to his prayer,
They swore to hale him forward by the hair
If he demurred, who, fiercely struggling, shook
His old notched crutch ; when Michael, with the
    look
Of a sick lion, groaned " Come, father, come,
Our country casts us forth, banished from hearth
    and home.

XXXV.

" God may have given the land to dress and keep
Unto our hands, but then his lordship's sheep
Fetch more i' the market. So with all our roots,
Like ill-weeds choking up the corn's young shoots,
He plucks us from the soil. His sovereign word
Hath driven us hence. As with a flaming sword
Doth he not bar the entrance to our glen ?
But, father, if we must, shall we not go like men ? "

7

XXXVI.

Then with his children Michael strode along,
His father followed through the elbowing throng
Of men and women, darting here and there
To snatch up children, or their household ware,
Splashing through sea pools, stumbling over blocks,
To where the boats banged sharply on the rocks,
Bobbing like corks, and bearing from the shore
Their freight of human souls towards the *Koh-i-noor*.

XXXVII.

But as the shout of sailors, as the stroke
And dip of oars upon his senses broke,
The old man started back, and 'mid the loud
Din and confusion of the pushing crowd
He disappeared unnoticed, as the ship,
With many a lunge and shake and roll and dip,
Now weighed her anchors, and with bulging sail
Close-reefed, and creaking shrouds, drove on before
    the gale.

XXXVIII.

And crowding on the decks, with hungry eyes
Straining towards the coast that flies and flies,
The crofters stand ; and whether with tears or foam
The faces fastened on their dwindling home
Are wet, they know not, as they lean and yearn
Over the trickling bulwark by the stern
Toward each creek and headland of that shore,
The long-loved lineaments they may see never more.

XXXIX.

Therewith it seemed as if their Scottish land
Bled for its children, yea, as though some hand—
Stretching from where on the horizon's verge
The rayless sun hung on the reddening surge—
Incarnadined the sweep of perilous coast
And the embattled storm-clouds swarthy host,
With such wild hues of mingling blood and fire
As though the heavens themselves flashed in
    celestial ire.

XL.

And in the kindling of that wrathful light
Their huts, yet flaming up from vale and height,
Grew pale as watch-fires in the glare of day ;
White constellated isles leagues far away,
Headlands and reefs and paps, whose fretted stone
Breasted the sucking whirlpool's clamorous moan,
Grew incandescent o'er the wind-flogged sea,
Scaled over with whitening scum as struck with
     leprosy.

XLI.

For as the winds blew up to hurricane,
Like a mere spark quenched on the curdled main
The ship was swept beyond the old man's sight,
A dizzy watcher on that lonesome height,
Where, grappled to a fragment of the keep,
He hung and swung high o'er the raging deep
While sea-gulls buffeted about his locks,
Slipped shrieking into chinks and crannies of the
     rocks.

XLII.

And now the waves that thundered on the shore
Him seemed the iron-throated cannon's roar ;
And now his heart, upstarting as from sleep,
Shuddered for those that sailed upon the deep,
As in brief flashes of his clouded mind
He knew himself sole crofter left behind
Of all his clan—crying now and again,
" She's cleared the Sound of Sleat—safe on the open
    main.

XLIII.

" She's safe now with the treacherous reefs behind ! "
He shouted, as in answer to the wind
That had swung round like some infuriate host,
With all its blasts set full upon the coast ;
And hounded back, the ship, as if at bay,
Came reeling through the twilight, thick and grey
With rags of solid foam and shock of breaking
Waters, beneath whose blows the very rocks were
    shaking.

XLIV.

Yea, near and nearer to the deadly shore
She pitches helpless 'mid the bellowing roar
Of confluent breakers, as with sidelong keel,
Dragging her anchors, she doth plunge and reel,
Dashed forwards, then recoiling from the rocks,
Whose flinty ribs ring to the Atlantic shocks—
On, on, and ever on, till hurled and battered
Sheer on the rock she springs, and falls back
        wrecked and shattered.

XLV.

And through the smoke of waters and the clouds
Of driving foam, boats, rigging, masts, and shrouds
Whirled round and round; and then athwart the
        storm
The old man saw, or raving saw, the form
Of his own son, as with his children pressed
Close to his heart, borne on the giddy crest
Of a sheer wall of wave, he rose and rose,
Then with the refluent surge rolled whelmed beneath
        its snows.

XLVI.

And through the lurid dusk and mist of spray
That quenched the last spark of the smouldering day,
Faces of drowning men were seen to swim
Amid the vortex, or a hand or limb
To push through whelming waters, or the scream
Wrung from a swimmer's choking lips would seem
To be borne in upon the reeling brain
Of that old man, who swooned beneath the mortal
    strain.

XLVII.

Yea, thus once more upon the natal coast,
Which, living, those brave hearts had left and lost,
The pitying winds and waves drove back to land,
If but to drown them by the tempest's hand,
The banished Highlanders.   Safe in the deep,
With their own seas to rock their hearts to sleep,
The crofters lay : but faithful Rory gave
His body to the land that had begrudged a grave.

NOTES.

DUAN SECOND, STANZA XVII., PAGE 37.

"OR quelle est la situation du Crofter de l'époque actuelle? Ce n' est plus qu' un fermier sans bail, dont la redevance est susceptible d'augmentations arbitraires, *et qui peut etre renvoyé d' un pour a' l'autre.* D'année en année, les limites du sol in grat et épuisé que les grands propriétaires abandonment á la petite culture deviennent de plus en plus restreintes. L' 'eviction' frappe sans pitié les humbles tenanciers dont les rangs se sont toujours éclaircis depuis un siécle dans les immenses domaines de la haute Ecosse. . . .

"La population des Crofters, des Highlands et des Iles, si peu importante qu'elle soit, est une pépinière de bons travailleurs et de bons citoyens pour tout l'empire. Par sa vigoureuse constitution physique, son intelligence native et sa bonne éducation morale, elle est particulièrement propre au recrutement du peuple dans les grands centres industriels, qui, s'il n'était alimenté de la sorte par les sources saines des districts ruraux, ne manquerait pas de dégénérer, sans l'influence des mauvais logements, d'occupations malsaines et d' habitudes énervantes. . . .

"Mais ce n' est pas seulement au point de vue de ces avantages particulieres qui la population des Crofters a une utilité indiscutable. Elle constitue une base naturelle pour la défense navale du pays, défense qui ne peut être improvisée et dont l'importance, dans certaines circonstances, ne saurait être estimée trop haut. La population maritime des Highlands et des Iles fournit, en ce moment, 4431 hommes à la réserve de la marine royale, nombre équivalent aux équipages de sept navires de guerre cuirassé de ıre classe, et qui pourrait être encore beaucoup accru au moyeu d' avantages proportionés.

"Il en est de même du recrutement de l'armée de terre. Les enrôlements deviennent de plus en plus rares dans les Highlands, l'émigration moissonant la partie la plus robuste et la plus determinée de la population rurale."—"*Les Highlands et la Question des Crofters*," *par Le Cte Louis Lafond.*

DUAN THIRD, STANZA XXVI., PAGE 55.

"The tenants of Knoydart, like all other Highlanders, had suffered severely during and after the potato famine in 1846 and 1847, and some of them got into arrear with a year's and some with two years' rent, but they were fast clearing it off. Mrs. Macdonell and her factor determined to evict every crofter on her property, to make room for sheep. In the spring of 1853 they were all served with summonses of removal, accompanied by a message that Sir John Macneil, Chairman of the Board of Supervision, had agreed to convey them to Australia. Their feelings were not considered worthy of the slightest consideration. They were not even asked whether they would prefer to follow their countrymen to America and Canada. They were to be treated as if they were nothing better than Africans, and the laws of their country on a level with those which regulated South American slavery. The people, however, had no alternative but to accept any offer made to them. They could not get an inch of land on any of the neighbouring estates, and any one who would give them a night's shelter was threatened with eviction themselves. It was afterwards found not convenient to transport them to Australia, and it was then intimated to the poor creatures, as if they were nothing but common slaves, to be disposed of at will, that they would be taken to North America, and that a ship would be at Isle Orsay, in the Island of Skye, in a few days to receive them, and that they *must* go on board. The *Sillery* soon arrived, and Mrs. Macdonell and her factor came all the way from Edinburgh to see the people hounded across in boats, and put on board this ship, whether they would or not. An eye-witness who described the proceeding at the time, in a now rare pamphlet, and whom I met last year at Nova Scotia, characterises the scene as indescribable and heart-rending. The wail of the poor women and children as they were torn away from their homes would have melted a heart of stone! Some few families, principally cottars, refused to go, in spite of every influence brought to bear upon them, and the treatment they afterwards received was cruel beyond belief. The houses, not only of those who went, but of those who remained, were burnt and levelled to the ground. The Strath was dotted all over with black spots, showing where yesterday stood the habitations of men. The scarred, half-burnt wood—couples, rafters, and bars—were strewn about in every direction. Stooks of corn and plots of unlifted potatoes could be seen on all sides, but man was gone. No voice could be heard. Those who refused to go aboard the *Sillery* were in hiding among the rocks and the caves, while their friends were packed off like so many African slaves to the Cuban market."—"*The Highland Clearances,*" by *Alexander Mackenzie* (pp. 267, 268).

DUAN THIRD, STANZA XXVI., PAGE 55.

"The clearing of Sutherland was a process of ruin so thoroughly disastrous that it might be deemed scarcely possible to render it more complete. Between the years 1811 and 1820, 15,000 inhabitants of this northern district were ejected from their snug inland farms by means for which we would seek in vain a precedent, except, perhaps, in the history of the Irish massacre. A singularly well-conditioned and wholesome district of country has been converted into one wide ulcer of wretchedness and woe."—*Hugh Miller.*

DUAN THIRD, STANZA XXVII., PAGE 55.

"Yearly the Highlands have sent forth their thousands from their glens to follow the battle-flag of Britain wherever it flew. It was a Highland *rearlorn* hope that followed the broken wreck of Cumberland's army after the disastrous day at Fontenoy, when more British soldiers lay dead upon the field than fell at Waterloo. It was another Highland regiment that scaled the rock-face over the St. Lawrence, and first formed a line in the September dawn on the level sward of Abraham. It was a Highland line that broke the power of the Mahratta hordes and gave Wellington his maiden victory at Assaye. Thirty-four battalions marched from these glens to fight in America, Germany, and India ere the eighteenth century had run its course; and yet while abroad over the earth Highlanders were the first in assault and the last in retreat, their lowly homes in far-away glens were being dragged down, and the wail of women and the cry of children went out on the same breeze that bore too upon its wings the scent of heather, the freshness of gorse blossom, and the myriad sweets that made the lowly life of Scotland's peasantry blest with health and happiness."—" *The Highland Clearances*," by *Alexander Mackenzie* (pages 320, 321).

" Few Englishmen even now seem to be aware, notwithstanding all that has been written on the subject, that not very long ago, in many instances within the memory of living men, most of the Highland counties were the scene of evictions on a wholesale scale, compared with which the forced emigration of the Irish peasantry sinks into insignificance. Entire communities, from the patriarch of two generations down to the newly-born babe, were banished *en bloc* to Canada, and thrown there on their own resources to establish new homes or to starve. And although the people, except in a few cases, submitted to expatriation quietly if unwillingly, where they did manifest any reluctance to accept their fate, their houses were burned down over their heads, and they themselves were turned adrift on the bleak hill-sides, and on the wild and inhospitable sea-shores of that northern region, to seek subsistence as best they could. Until 1745, the year of Culloden, the clan system of land tenure prevailed in the Highlands, under which the ground belonged not to the chief alone, but to the community. A clansman could not be dispossessed of his holding by his chief. After 1745, however, the English system was introduced. The clans that had remained loyal to the Crown, as well as those that had thrown in their lot with Prince Charles, had their lands practically confiscated. The Highland chiefs, in short, were assimilated in position to English landlords. They were by the central government invested with the fee-simple of the land which was once held by the laird and the clansmen in common, and so a great wrong, amounting to a national crime, was done to the Highland population."—"*Storm-Clouds in the Highlands.*" *J. A. Cameron.* "*Nineteenth Century,*" *Sept.* 1884.

"I know a glen, now inhabited by two shepherds and two gamekeepers, which at one time sent out its thousand fighting men. And this is but one of many that might be cited to show how the Highlands have been depopulated. Loyal, peaceable, and high-spirited peasantry have been driven from their native land—as the Jews were expelled from Spain, or the Huguenots from France—to make room for grouse, sheep, and deer. A portly volume would be needed to contain the records of oppression and cruelty perpetrated by many landlords, who are a scourge to their unfortunate tenants, blighting their lives, poisoning their happiness, and robbing them of their improvements, filling their wretched homes with sorrow, and breaking their hearts with the weight of despair."—*Dr. D. G. F. Macdonald.*

"We come now to the third stage in the history of land-lordism in the Highlands—the stage which I have distinguished as that of the Nineteenth Century Clearances. In consequence of the English clearances of the sixteenth century, the spread of commercial principles, and the dying out of the old notion and fact of collective and limited ownership of land, the notion of individual and absolute ownership had got pretty well established in England by the middle of last century. So, after the Rebellion of 1745, the Highland chiefs being greatly impoverished, the devil came to them in three different shapes, one after another. First he appeared in a guise he very often assumes—the guise of a pressing creditor ; then he came as a jolly sheep-farmer from the south, with lots of tin in his pockets ; and, said the jolly sheep-farmer to the impecunious Highland chief : ' Clear out these —— rascals, who call themselves your clansmen. Sheep will pay you better than men, and if you will let the hills and glens to me, I'll double, triple, quadruple your rental.' And last of all the devil came to the Highland chief in another shape he very often assumes—that of a sharp lawyer. The chiefs knew very well that they were but joint-owners with their clans of the land they occupied, and that crofter townships had rights of grazing on the hills sanctioned by immemorial custom ; and they knew very well that, though many a chief's estate had been forfeited by Acts of Attainder, by no Act of Parliament had their clansmen's customary rights been forfeited. ' But,' said the devil in the shape of the sharp lawyer, 'never mind that. In England they act now on the notion of absolute ownership, and we'll just assume that your people are tenants-at-will, and that you can do what you like with them and theirs.' And it was simply on this assumption, a pure legal fiction, directly in the teeth of all historical facts, that the Duke of Athole began the Highland Clearances in clearing Glen Tilt, just one hundred years ago (1784), and worthily have followed suit the Dukes of Sutherland and of Argyll."—*Article on " The Crofters' Revolt," by J. S. Stuart Glennie, in " Our Corner"* (p. 202).

DUAN THIRD, STANZA XXVIII., PAGE 56.

In his recent work on the Nationalisation of Land, Mr. Alfred Russell Wallace, in the chapter on " Landlordism in Scotland," writes :—" The facts stated in this chapter will possess, I feel sure, for many Englishmen, an almost startling novelty ; the tale of oppression and cruelty they reveal reads like one of those hideous stories peculiar to the dark ages, rather than a simple record of events happening upon our own land and within the memory of the present generation. For a parallel to this mon-strous power of the land-owner, under which life and property are entirely at his mercy, we must go back to mediæval times, or to the days when serfdom not having been abolished, the Russian noble was armed with despotic authority ; while the more pitiful results of this landlord tyranny, the wide devastation of culti-vated lands, the heartless burning of houses, the reckless creation of pauperism and misery out of well-being and con-tentment, could only be expected under the rule of Turkish Sultans, or greedy and cruel Pashas. Yet these cruel deeds have been perpetrated in one of the most beautiful portions of our native land. They are not the work of uncultured bar-barians or of fanatic Moslems, but of so-called civilised and Christian men ; and—worst feature of all—they are not due to any high-handed exercise of power beyond the law, but are strictly legal, are in many cases the acts of the legislature itself. . . . The general results of the system of modern land-lordism in Scotland are not less painful than the hardship and misery brought upon individual sufferers. The earlier improvers, who drove the peasants from their sheltered valleys to the exposed sea-coast, in order to make room for sheep-farmers, pleaded erroneously the public benefit as the justification of their conduct. They maintained that more food and clothing would be produced by the new system, and that the people themselves would have the advantage of the produce of the sea as well as that of the land for their support. The result, however, proved them to be mistaken, for thenceforth the cry of Highland destitution began to be heard, culminating at intervals into actual famines, like that of 1836-37, when £70,000 were distributed to keep the Highlanders from death by starvation. . . . Just as in Ireland, there was abundance of land capable of cultivation, but the people were driven to the coast and to the towns to make way for sheep, and cattle, and lowland farmers ; and when the barren and inhospitable tracts allotted to them became overcrowded, they were told to emigrate.

" The actual effect of this system of eviction and emigration— of banishing the native of the soil and giving it to the stranger —is shown in the steady increase of poverty, indicated by the amount spent for the relief of the poor having increased from less than £300,000 in 1846 to more than £900,000 now ; while in the same period the population has only increased from 2,770,000 to 3,627,000, so that pauperism has grown about nine times faster than population. . . .

" At the present time more than two million acres of Scottish soil are devoted to the preservation of deer alone—an area larger than the entire counties of Kent and Surrey combined. Glen Tilt Forest includes 100,000 acres ; the Black Mount is sixty miles in circumference ; and Ben Aulder Forest is fifteen miles long by seven broad. On many of these forests there is the finest pasture in Scotland, while the valleys would support a considerable population of small farmers ; yet all this land is devoted to the sport of the wealthy, farms being destroyed, houses pulled down, and men, sheep, and cattle all banished to create a wilderness for the deer-stalkers! At the same time the whole people of England are shut out from many of the grandest and most interesting scenes of their native land, gamekeepers and watchers forbidding the tourist or naturalist to trespass on some of the wildest Scotch mountains."

"The cruel practice of evicting the Highlanders to make room for sheep seems to be passing into the pernicious system of *converting grazing lands into sporting grounds.* Only the other day an extensive tract was cleared of 7000 sheep to add to the already wide forests of Glenstrathfarar and Culligran, the property of Lord Lovat, let to Mr. Winans of Brighton, at £7000 per annum. It is said that this nobleman, being desirous of securing more broad acres for his American "Sportsman!" who boasts of having, with the help of his two sons, brought down twenty-seven stags in about an hour last September, has leased the sheep-farm in question at a rent of £1000 a-year, and sub-let it to Mr. Winans for £2000, thus netting £1000 per annum by the transaction. I blush to think that a Scottish nobleman should lend himself to satisfying the insatiable desire of a foreign millionaire contractor to make a profit by a system which depopulates the Highlands, is a curse to Scotland, and, as you very properly observed, 'a scandal to British legislation.'

"Sad is it to see the rights and welfare of the Highlanders pitilessly disregarded, and the beautiful hills, straths, and glens of Scotland immolated to the sporting snobbishness of greedy capitalists. The existence of 'mammoth deer-forests' is one of the gravest wrongs of the people, perpetrated under the mask of a false political economy, and I defy anyone to prove the utility of the cruel clearances that have so scandalised the Northern Highlands.

" We may wander whither we will, the busy life that once enlivened these solitudes has departed. The cots are bare, and cold, and roofless ; the patches which once grew crops of golden corn are now absorbed by sporting playgrounds ; voices of men, women, and children no longer echo from the surrounding hills --nought but barren solitary pomp

‘ Where once a garden smiled.’

Family after family have been chased away, leaving us to saddening memories of the past."—D. G. F. MACDONALD, LL.D. —" *The Echo*," 1878.

DUAN THIRD, STANZA XLIV., PAGE 64.

" In former removals the tenants had been allowed to carry away the timber of their old dwellings to erect houses on their new allotments, but now a more summary mode was adopted by setting fire to them. The able-bodied men were by this time away after their cattle, or otherwise engaged at a distance, so that the immediate sufferers by the general house-burning that now commenced were the aged and infirm, the women and children. . . . The devastators proceeded with the greatest celerity, demolishing all before them ; and when they had overthrown all the houses in a large tract of country, they set fire to the wreck. Timber, furniture, and every other article that could not be instantly removed was consumed by fire, or otherwise utterly destroyed. The proceedings were carried on with the greatest rapidity and the most reckless cruelty. Some old men took to the woods and the rocks, wandering about in a state approaching to or of absolute insanity ; and several of them in this situation lived only a few days. Pregnant women were taken in premature labour, and several children did not long survive their sufferings. To those scenes I was an eye-witness, and am ready to substantiate the truth of my statements, not only by my own testimony, but by that of many others who were present at the time. In such a scene of devastation it is almost useless to particularise the cases of individuals : the suffering was great and universal. I shall, however, notice a very few of the extreme cases, of which I was myself an eye-witness. John Mackay's wife, Ravigill, in attempting to pull down her house, in the absence of her husband, to preserve the timber, fell through the roof. She was in consequence taken in premature labour, and in that state was exposed to the open air and to the view of all the bystanders. Donald Munro, Garvott, lying in a fever, was turned out of his house and exposed to the elements. Donald Macbeath, an infirm and bed-ridden old man, had the house unroofed over him, and was in that state exposed to the wind and rain until death put a period to his sufferings. I was present at the pulling down and burning of the house of William Chisholme, Badinloskin, in which was lying his wife's mother, an old bed-ridden woman of nearly one hundred years of age, none of the family being present. . . . Fire was set to the house, and the blankets in which she was carried out were in flames before she could be got out. She was placed in a little shed, and it was with great difficulty they were prevented from firing it also. Within five days she was a corpse."—"*Gloomy Memories,*" *by Donald Macleod.*

Duan Third, Stanza lxii., Page 73.

"As Strathnaver, though from many causes the most widely bruited, was by no means a solitary instance of rash reform and harsh procedure, we must give another example of the same ruthless process of extermination which took place some forty years later in a quite different region. We allude to the inhab-itants of the district of Knoydart, who were cleared out of their native seats in the year 1853, in a fashion for which the Strathnaver procedure seemed to have formed the model, and of which an account is given by Donald Ross, an eye-witness.

" ' The scene presented at Knoydart was most heart-rending. As far as the eye could see the face of the strath had its black spots, where the houses of the crofters were either levelled or burnt. The ruins of these habitations of men, and the silence and solitude that prevailed, rendered it unnecessary for any tongue to tell me that here humanity was most cruelly sacrificed to the god of sheep-farming and expatriation. The blackened rafters lying scattered among the grass, the couple-trees cut through the middle and thrown away, the walls broken down, thatch and cabers mixed up together, and grass beginning to grow on the threshold and hearthstone, told a tale which re-quired neither tongue nor pen to unfold. The scene was rendered more painful as the Strath was dotted with stacks of corn, large plots of potatoes, and with grass that could be easily mowed down by the scythe. But the voice of man was gone— he was not to be found.' "—" *The Scottish Highlanders and the Land Laws,*" *by Professor Blackie.*

"The extermination of the Highlanders has been carried on for many years as systematically and relentlessly as of the North American Indians. . . . Who can withhold sympathy, as whole families have turned to take a last look at the heavens red with their burning houses? The poor people shed no tears, for there was in their hearts that which stifled such signs of emotion; they were absorbed in despair. They were forced away from that which was near and dear to their hearts, and their patriotism was treated with contemptuous mockery."—*Dr. D. G. F. Macdonald.*

DUAN THIRD, STANZA LXIII, PAGE 73.

"Among the rest, a young man, Donald MacKay, of Grambinor, was ordered out of his parents' house; he obeyed in a state of delirium, and (nearly naked) ran into some bushes adjoining, where he lay for a considerable time deprived of reason; the house was immediately in flames, and his effects burned. Robert MacKay, whose whole family were in the fever, or otherwise ailing, had to carry his two daughters on his back a distance of about twenty-five miles. . . . A number of the sick, who could not be carried away instantly, on account of their dangerous situation, were collected by their friends and placed in an uncomfortable hut, and there for a time left to their fate. The cries of these victims were heart-rending—exclaiming in their anguish, 'Are you going to leave us to perish in the flames?' . . . It may not be out of place here to mention generally that the clergy, factors, and magistrates were cool and apparently unconcerned spectators of the scenes I have been describing, which were indeed perpetrated under their immediate authority. The splendid and comfortable mansions of these gentlemen were reddened with the glare of their neighbours' flaming houses, without exciting any compassion for the sufferers; no spiritual, temporal, or medical aid was afforded them; and this time they were all driven away without being allowed the benefit of their out-going crops! Nothing but the sword was wanting to make the scene one of as great barbarity as the earth ever witnessed; and in my opinion, this would, in a majority of cases, have been mercy, by saving them from what they were afterwards doomed to endure. The clergy indeed, in their sermons, maintained that the whole was a merciful interposition of Providence to bring them to repentance, rather than to send them all to hell, as they so richly deserved."—" *The Highland Clearances,*" *by Alexander Mackenzie* (p. 30).

DUAN FOURTH, STANZA V., PAGE 76.

One of the Royal Commissioners remarked—" It is said in reference to the people that 'they were compelled to emigrate to America; some of them had been tied before our eyes; others hid themselves in caves and crevices for fear of being caught by authorised officers.'

"*Q.*—' Do you recall that these people were caught and sent to America, just like an animal going to market?'

"*A.*—'Just the same way. I saw a man who lay down on his face and knees on a little island to hide himself from the policeman, *who had dogs searching for him* in order to get him aboard the emigrant ship. . . . There was another case of a man named Angus Johnson. He had a dead child in the house, and his wife gave birth to three children, all of whom died. Not-

withstanding this he was seized and tied on the pier at Loch Bois-
dale, and *kicked* on board. The old priest interfered and said,
'What are you doing to this man? let him alone, it is against
the law!' The wife of the man who was tied and put aboard
afterwards went to the vessel. The four dead children would be
buried by that time. *These things happened in the years* 1850–
51. The people were hiding themselves in caves and dens for
fear of being sent away from the island. . . . There were
many such cases at the time. It was about forty years ago."
—"*Crofters' Evidence," given before the Royal Commission.*

DUAN FOURTH, STANZA XXVII., PAGE 87.

"All the Highlanders of an inland district in Sutherlandshire
were ejected from their homes by the late Duke to make way
for a few *sheep-farmers.* The poor people, a moral and religious
race, bound to their rugged hills with a strength of attachment
hardly equalled in any other country, could not be made to
believe the summonses of removal real. Their fathers had lived
and died among those very hills for thousands of years. They
had spent their blood and had laid down their lives of old for
the good Earls of Sutherland. Could it be possible that they
were to be forced out of their own country? They at first
thought of resistance, and had they carried the thought into
action, it would have afforded perilous employment to
a thousand armed men to have ejected every eight
hundred of them; but they had read their New Testa-
ments, and they knew that the Duke had become pro-
prietor of the soil; some of their houses were actually fired over
their heads, and yet there was no bloodshed. Convinced at

length that no other alternative remained for them, they gathered in a body in the churchyard of the district, to take leave of their country for ever, and of the dust of their fathers' last. And there, seated among the graves, men and women, the old and the young, with one accord, and under the influence of one feeling, 'lifted up their voices and wept.' This tract of the Highlands is now inhabited by sheep."—*Hugh Miller*.

DUAN FOURTH, STANZA XXXI., PAGE 89.

" We, the undersigned, passengers per *Admiral*, from Storno-way, in the Highlands of Scotland, do solemnly depose to the following facts :—That Colonel Gordon is proprietor of estates in South Uist of Barra ; that among many hundred tenants and cottars whom he has sent this season from his estates to Canada, he gave directions to his factor, Mr. Fleming, of Cluny Castle, Aberdeenshire, to ship on board of the above-named vessel a number of nearly four hundred and fifty of said tenants and cottars, from the estate in Barra ; that accordingly, a great majority of these people, among whom were the undersigned, proceeded voluntarily to embark on board the *Admiral* at Loch Boisdale, on or about 11th August 1851 ; but that several of the people who were intended to be shipped for this port, Quebec, refused to proceed on board, and, in fact, absconded from their homes to avoid the embarkation. Whereupon Mr. Fleming gave orders to a policeman, who was accompanied by a ground-officer of the estate in Barra, and some constables, to pursue the people who had run away among the mountains ; which they did, and succeeded in capturing about twenty from the mountains and islands in the neighbourhood ; but only came with the officers on an attempt being made to handcuff them ; and that some who ran away were not brought back, in consequence of which four families at least were divided, some having come in the ships to Quebec, while other members of the same families are left in the Highlands. . . .

" The undersigned finally declare that they are now landed in Qeubec so destitute that, if immediate relief be not afforded them, and continued until they are settled in employment, they will be liable to perish with want. (*Signed*) HECTOR LAMONT, *and seventy others."*—" *The Highland Clearances,"* by *Alexander Mackenzie* (pp. 257, 258).

DUAN FOURTH, STANZA XV., PAGE 91.

" In too many instances the Highlands have been drained, not of their superfluity of population, but of the whole mass of the inhabitants, dispossessed by an unrelenting avarice, which will be one day found to have been as short-sighted as it is unjust and selfish.   Meantime, the Highlands may become the fairy-ground for romance and poetry, or the subject of experiment for the professors of speculation, political and economical.   But if the hour of need should come—and it may not, perhaps, be far distant—the pibroch may sound through the deserted region, but the summons will remain unanswered." —*Sir Walter Scott.*

DUAN FOURTH, STANZA XXXVIII., PAGE 93.

" Men talk of the Sutherland clearings as if they stood alone amidst the atrocities of the system ; but those who know fully the facts of the case can speak with as much truth of Ross-shire

clearings, the Inverness-shire clearings, the Perthshire clear-
ings, and, to some extent, the Argyleshire clearings. . . .
Crossing to the south of the great glen, we may begin with
Glencoe. How much of its romantic interest does the glen owe
to its desolation ? Let us remember, however, that the desola-
tion, in a large part of it, is the result of the extrusion of its
inhabitants. Travel eastward and the footprints of the destroyer
cannot be lost sight of. Large tracts along the Spean and its
tributaries are a wide waste. The southern bank of Loch
Lochy is almost without inhabitants, though the symptoms
of former occupancy are frequent. When we enter the
country of the Frasers, the same spectacle presents itself—a
desolate land. Trace the Beauly through all its upper reaches,
and how many thousands upon thousands of acres, once peopled,
are, as respects human beings, a wild wilderness. . . . Suther-
land, with all its atrocities, affords but a fraction of the atrocities
that have been perpetrated in following out the ejectment
system of the Highlands. In truth, of the habitable portion of
the whole country, but a small part is now really inhabited.

"Let us leave the past, however, and consider the present,
and it is a melancholy reflection that the year 1849 has added
its long list of Highland ejectments. While the law is banish-
ing its tens for terms of seven or fourteen years, as the penalty of
deep-dyed crimes, irresponsible and infatuated power is banish-
ing its thousands for life for no crime whatever."—*Hugh Miller :
"The Witness."*

Printed by WALTER SCOTT, *Felling, Newcastle-on-Tyne.*

THE CAMELOT CLASSICS.

New Comprehensive Edition of the Leading Prose Writers.
Edited by ERNEST RHYS.

In SHILLING Monthly Volumes, Crown 8vo; each Volume containing about 400 pages, clearly printed on good paper, and strongly bound in cloth.

PROSPECTUS.

THE main idea in instituting this Edition is to provide the general reader with a comprehensive Prose Library after his own heart,—an Edition, that is to say, cheap, without the reproach which cheapness usually implies, comprising volumes of shapely form, well printed, well bound, and thoroughly representative of the leading prose writers of all time. Placed thus upon a popular basis, making the principle of literary selection a broadly human rather than an academic one, the Edition will, the Publisher hopes, contest not ineffectually the critical suffrages of the democratic shilling.

As in the CANTERBURY POETS issued from the same press, to which this aims at being a companion series, the *Editing* of the volumes will be a special feature. This will be entrusted to writers who will each, in freshly-treated, suggestive Introductions, give just that account of the book and its author which will enable the significance of both in life and literature, and their relation to modern thought, to be readily grasped. And where, for the successful rescue of old-time books for modern reading, revision and selection are necessary, the editing will be done with careful zeal and with reverence always for the true spirit of the book.

LONDON:
WALTER SCOTT, 24 WARWICK LANE, PATERNOSTER ROW.

THE CAMELOT CLASSICS.

The Series is issued in two styles of Binding—Red Cloth, Cut
Edges ; and Dark Blue Cloth, Uncut Edges. Either Style, PRICE
ONE SHILLING.

The Canterbury Poets.

NOW READY, PRICE ONE SHILLING,

SONNETS OF THIS CENTURY.

*With an Exhaustive and Critical Essay
on the Sonnet.*

By WILLIAM SHARP.

SONNETS BY

Lord Tennyson.	Edward Dowden.
Robert Browning.	Edmund Gosse.
A. C. Swinburne.	Andrew Lang.
Matthew Arnold.	George Meredith.
Theodore Watts.	Cardinal Newman.
Archbishop Trench.	BY THE LATE
J. Addington Symonds.	Dante Gabriel Rossetti.
W. Bell Scott.	Mrs. Barrett Browning.
Christina Rossetti.	C. Tennyson-Turner, etc.

And all the Best Writers of the Century.

LONDON :
WALTER SCOTT, 24 Warwick Lane, Paternoster Row.